Ready for Kindergarten

written by Bethany V. Freitas • illustrated by Maja Andersen

Clarion Books

An Imprint of

HarperCollins Publishers

Look who's ready for kindergarten.
It's you!

In kindergarten, you'll practice
what you can do and learn
some new things, too.

Ready to see what I mean?

Have you ever tried to point to your head, shoulders, knees, and toes?

If you know your body,
you are ready for kindergarten.

You listen to stories
(and make up some of your own!).

With your big imagination,
you are ready for kindergarten.

You create art with scissors,
paint, paper, and glue.

If you're into making
beautiful messes,
you are ready for kindergarten.

Count the shoes on your feet.
Count the stairs going down.

You have fun with numbers.
You are ready for kindergarten.

Circle wheels, triangle roofs, rectangle doors.
What other shapes can you find?

You see shapes in your world.
You are ready for kindergarten.

KINDERGARTEN

You play with letters.

You are ready for kindergarten.

Skipping, zooming, digging, swinging.
You like to move with friends.

You are always on the go.
You are ready for kindergarten.

You know your name. You can say it out loud.
Get ready to introduce yourself to
your new teacher and friends.

Because look out, kindergarten . . .

. . . you are ready!

Ready to learn, ready to explore,

ready to try new things.

You are ready to have fun.

You are ready for kindergarten!

A Note to Caregivers

Beginning kindergarten can be exciting and scary for kids and for the adults who love them. Often, children find themselves asking, "Am I ready?" Whether they are attending school for the first time or making the leap to "big kid school," kindergarten is a place where kids will develop their language, social, and literacy skills in leaps and bounds.

Here are some ways to set your child up for kindergarten success:

★ Read this book (and others!) in a lively voice, showing your child how excited you are about books and reading. Take time on each page to read the words and talk about the pictures.

★ Invite your child to "read" the pictures to you. Ask questions such as "Can you count the clouds in the sky?" and "How is this child getting ready for kindergarten?"

★ Reread this book (and others!). Repetition helps children learn how books and stories work and creates a familiar routine around reading.

★ Practice the activities and skills in the book with your child. Make them part of your day-to-day and have fun!

★ Help your child practice introducing themselves, including saying their name clearly and correcting others' pronunciation. Some families enjoy sharing stories with their children of how they got their names— this builds interest and confidence.

★ Use this book to have conversations about meeting new people. Provide children with support for making friends with kids who may be different from themselves.

★ Talk with your child about any feelings they have around starting school. Help them see that there is space for all kinds of kids in kindergarten, no matter what they enjoy, what skills they have, and what things may still be tricky for them.

Now that you know the skills that kindergarten educators build upon right from the start, and ways to practice them with your child, our hope is that this book will leave you all feeling . . .

"Ready for Kindergarten!"

Molly Picardi, Staff Developer & Classroom Libraries Specialist, Teachers College Reading and Writing Project

Shanna Schwartz, Curriculum Coordinator for Primary Literacy, Teachers College Reading and Writing Project

For Teddy and Henry, who are ready for anything! —B.V.F.

I dedicate this book to all kindergarteners and their new adventures! —M.A.